A Dragon in the Sky

A Dragon in the Sky

THE STORY OF A GREEN DARNER DRAGONFLY

by Laurence Pringle

paintings by Bob Marstall

ORCHARD BOOKS : NEW YORK
An Imprint of Scholastic Inc.

To my good friend Dr. David Brown, teacher, farmer, auctioneer, and guide to the swamp near Sherman, New York, which was the perfect wetland for the beginning of a green darner's life.

—L.P.

For Faith Deering, whose love of insects is matched only by her excitement in learning new things about them. Her enthusiasm, encouragement, and tireless research were a major source of inspiration and support throughout my work on this book.

—B.M.

Text copyright © 2001 by Laurence Pringle
Paintings copyright © 2001 by Bob Marstall

Orchard Books, an imprint of Scholastic Inc.
95 Madison Avenue, New York, NY 10016

Manufactured in China
Printed by Toppan Printing Company, Inc.
Book design by Mina Greenstein
The text of this book is set in 12 point New Baskerville.
The paintings are rendered in watercolors and oil paints.

10 9 8 7 6 5 4 3 2 1

Library of Congress Cataloging-in-Publication Data
Pringle, Laurence P.
A dragon in the sky : the story of a green darner dragonfly /
by Laurence Pringle ; illustrated by Bob Marstall.
p. cm.
Includes bibliographical references and index.
Summary: Introduces the life cycle, feeding habits, migration, predators, and mating of the green darner dragonfly through the observation of one particular green darner named Anax.
ISBN 0-531-30315-2 (alk. paper)
1. Green darner—Juvenile literature. [1. Dragonflies.]
I. Marstall, Bob, ill. II. Title.
QL520.3.A4 P75 2001 595.7'33—dc21   00-39156

ACKNOWLEDGMENTS

For their knowledge of the facts, and mysteries, of dragonfly life and for their generous help, we thank many people, especially Michael May, Department of Entomology at Rutgers University, and Kenneth Soltesz, Westchester County Department of Parks, Recreation, and Conservation, who both became involved in the early stages of this project and who corrected errors in the text and sketches. We also thank Robert Barber of Rutgers University; Virginia Carpenter of the Nature Conservancy; Vincent Elia of the Cape May Bird Observatory; Faith Deering and Nathan Erwin of the O. Orkin Insect Zoo, National Museum of Natural History; Karen Frolich of the New York State Biodiversity Research Institute; David Gibo of the University of Toronto; Laurie Goodrich of Hawk Mountain Sanctuary Association; Christopher Letts of the Hudson River Foundation; Michael Meetz of Iowa State University; Richard Orr of the U.S. Department of Agriculture; Aleta Ringiero of Arizona State University; Laura Sirot of the University of Florida; as well as field naturalists Fred Morrison and Laurie Sanders of Massachusetts and Frank Nicolleti of Minnesota. Special thanks go to Nadja Andrasev for her timely assistance. Finally, we thank Hans Teensma, whose striking design of *An Extraordinary Life: The Story of a Monarch Butterfly* served to inform and inspire this companion book.

—*Laurence Pringle and Bob Marstall*

Anax's Journey

Sherman

Hawk
Mountain

Cape May

Chesapeake
Bay Bridge

Eastern United States

Cape Fear

Savannah

Contents

OVERLEAF:
The story begins in spring, in a swamp in western New York State.

A Swamp in the Spring

*B*EAVERS created the little swamp in far western New York State. They built a small dam in exactly the right place. It blocked the opening of a culvert that carried a tiny brook under the gravel country road. The water rose behind the dam and spread through the woods.

The beavers thrived there for a time, but now they and most of their dam were gone. A shallow swamp remained. The wetland was studded with the skeletons of trees that had died from too much water, but it was rich nonetheless in living plants and animals. A wetland in mid-May bursts with life—and the promise of even more life to come.

At night a chorus of frogs and toads overwhelmed all other sounds. Bullfrogs sounded their deep *jug-o-rums.* Green frogs twanged their bango-string calls. American toads trilled. Now it was morning, and most of the amphibian mating symphony was silent. Phoebes, red-winged blackbirds, and crows called. A pair of tree swallows twittered as they explored a hole in a dead maple—possibly a safe nest site in which to raise a family.

The little swamp is located in New York just nine miles north of the Pennsylvania border and four miles from Sherman, a small farming community. Some of the area's farms are owned by Amish families, who still use horses for transportation and farmwork. Six miles north of the swamp lies the Chautauqua Institution, a summer cultural center by Chautauqua Lake.

11

Two dragonflies, a male and a female, flew along the water's edge. They were green darners, among the biggest dragonflies of North America. Though still strong and able fliers, both showed signs of wear and tear—and for good reason. Just two months earlier they had begun their adult life in the deep South. Emerging from separate ponds, the green darners had each flown northward more than eight hundred miles. And now they had met and mated in the air over an unnamed swamp near Sherman, New York.

The male hovered above the female. He dipped down and grabbed his mate behind her head with claspers at the end of his

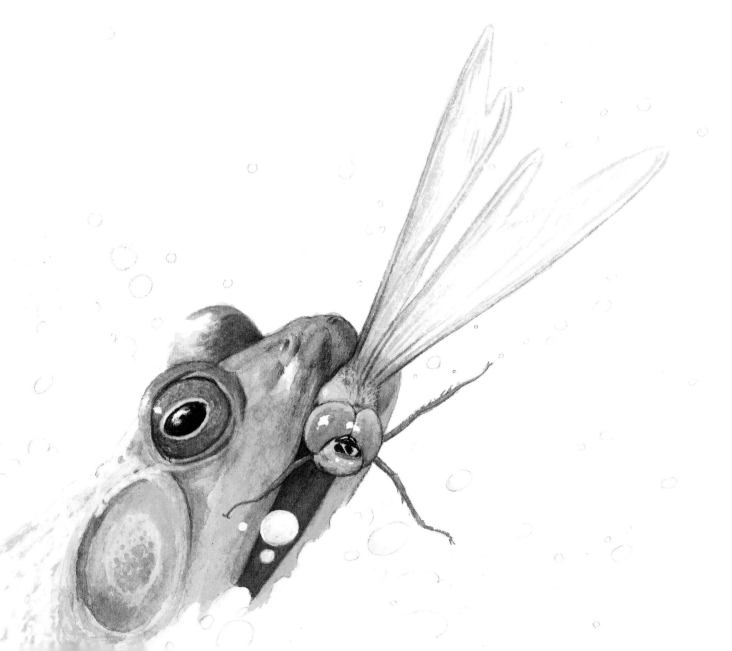

abdomen. The
green darners flew
that way for a while, in
tandem. Together they landed
on some cattail leaves at the edge of the
swamp. The female grasped a leaf, then backed down until
her abdomen was half underwater. Then, with the tip of
her abdomen, she slit a hole in the leaf. She pushed an egg
partway into the slit.

The female landed again and again on leaves that
emerged from the water, laying dozens of eggs, always with
her mate clutching the plants just above her. Both male and
female were alert for danger. Their sharp eyes scanned the
sky for a kingbird or other predator that ate dragonflies.
Neither darner noticed a slight disturbance in the water.
Neither noticed a dark underwater shape moving closer,
closer—until it was too late. The bullfrog lunged from
below. Its mouth engulfed the female dragonfly. The
male broke free and darted away. He returned a
moment later, scanning the swamp edge for his mate.
Faint ripples spread out over the water's surface.
That was all. There was no sign of her.

Beneath the surface, the bullfrog's digestive juices
had begun to work on the female green darner. She was
dead, but she had left hundreds of fertilized eggs. She would
be the mother of a whole new generation of green darner
dragonflies.

Darners are a group of large, fast-flying dragonflies. They were named darners because their long slender bodies resemble darning needles— long needles used to mend cloth by weaving thread or yarn across a tear or hole. Long ago in some farm families, naughty children were warned that their lips would be sewed shut by the "devil's darning needles"— dragonflies. These insects were also once called "mule killers" or "snake doctors," despite their inability to harm or help such animals.

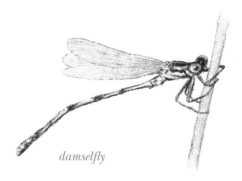

damselfly

Compared with dragonflies, most damselflies are small, dainty, and weak fliers. They also differ in the way they hold their wings at rest. Dragonflies spread their wings flat, like an airplane; damselflies usually fold theirs back, parallel to their bodies. Also, there is a space between the eyes of damselflies while the big eyes of dragonflies touch or have only a narrow space between them.

Dragonflies and damselflies were named Odonata by an eighteenth-century Danish entomologist, Johann Fabricius. The Greek word odon means "tooth," and Odonata means "tooth jawed." Both young and adult dragonflies have biting mouthparts that can give a harmless pinch to fingers but are deadly to mosquitoes, flies, and other small prey.

Dragonflies are remarkable creatures, with perhaps the sharpest vision of all insects and with flying ability that is admired by aeronautical engineers. Dragonflies are closely related to damselflies and, along with them, are classified in the order Odonata. There are more than fifty-seven hundred kinds of dragonflies and damselflies worldwide. Nearly five hundred species live in North America. They vary greatly in their color, size, behavior, habitat, and range.

One dragonfly in particular stands out among all of the Odonata: the green darner. It is the most common and widespread large dragonfly in North America. It lives in all fifty states, including Hawaii, and also in Tahiti, the West Indies, and parts of China. With a wingspan of five inches, this large blue-and-green dragonfly of swift flight can migrate more than a thousand miles. The green darner has a simple but powerful scientific name: *Anax junius*. Its name means "lord and master of June."

Before she died, the female green darner had laid several hundred eggs. They were shaped like tiny cucumbers, each about a millimeter long, or less than one-sixteenth of an inch. Cream colored at first, they soon turned reddish brown. Each egg had the potential of developing and growing to be an adult dragonfly. But nature creates and spends life lavishly. Some of the eggs would never hatch. Most of the young that did emerge from their eggs would be gobbled up by predators that stalked the underwater world of the swamp.

Only a few young would survive to soar into the sky as green darner dragonflies. One was a male, Anax. As an embryo within the egg, he developed slowly at first; the swamp water surrounding the egg was still chilly from the long winter. Then southern winds carried a taste of summer to western New York. Several days of unusually warm weather caused the water temperature to rise. The embryo within the egg developed more quickly.

One day, after about three weeks in the water, the egg began to quiver. A tiny creature emerged from one end—Anax had broken free. His body was slender. His legs were pressed against his body and were not completely formed. This first stage lasted for less than an hour. Then the creature, called a protonymph, split open along its back and Anax wriggled out as a dragonfly nymph.

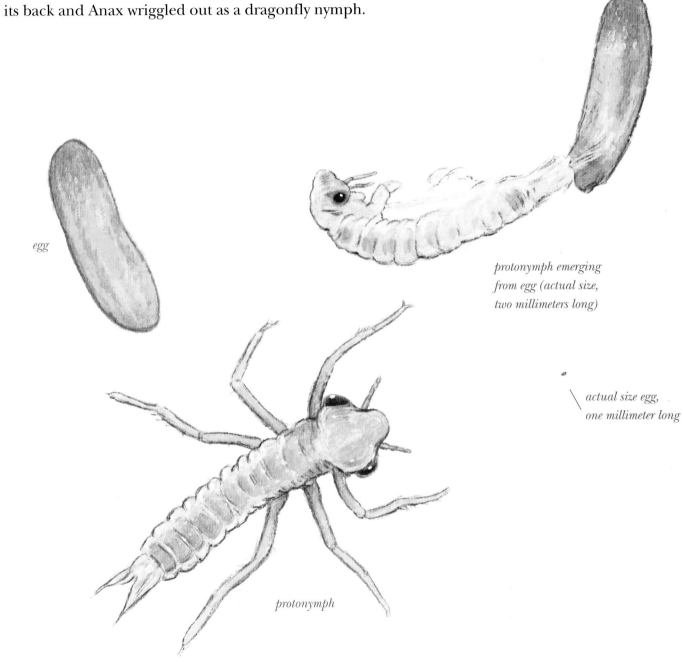

egg

protonymph emerging from egg (actual size, two millimeters long)

actual size egg, one millimeter long

protonymph

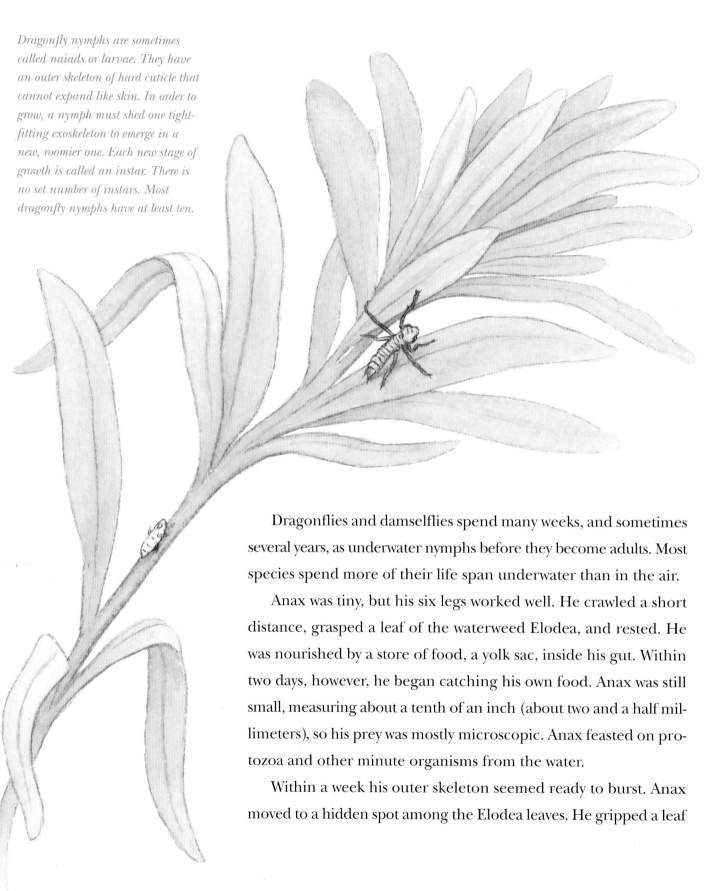

Dragonfly nymphs are sometimes called naiads or larvae. They have an outer skeleton of hard cuticle that cannot expand like skin. In order to grow, a nymph must shed one tight-fitting exoskeleton to emerge in a new, roomier one. Each new stage of growth is called an instar. There is no set number of instars. Most dragonfly nymphs have at least ten.

Dragonflies and damselflies spend many weeks, and sometimes several years, as underwater nymphs before they become adults. Most species spend more of their life span underwater than in the air.

Anax was tiny, but his six legs worked well. He crawled a short distance, grasped a leaf of the waterweed Elodea, and rested. He was nourished by a store of food, a yolk sac, inside his gut. Within two days, however, he began catching his own food. Anax was still small, measuring about a tenth of an inch (about two and a half millimeters), so his prey was mostly microscopic. Anax feasted on protozoa and other minute organisms from the water.

Within a week his outer skeleton seemed ready to burst. Anax moved to a hidden spot among the Elodea leaves. He gripped a leaf tightly with the hooks on the tips of his legs. Anax caused the blood pressure within his thorax to increase. The pressure from within grew and grew. The exoskeleton of his thorax bulged, then split down the middle. A new version of Anax began to emerge. Anax struggled and rested, struggled again, and finally freed himself. His second exoskeleton was twice the size of his first nymph "skin." Now an empty shell, it still clung tightly to a leaf. Anax moved away from it.

Anax had successfully molted, his only way of growing. He would molt ten more times before becoming a full-grown nymph.

His new exoskeleton was soft and green colored, but it soon hardened and darkened. Anax was almost invisible among the leaves. But by moving, Anax had attracted the attention of another swamp dweller.

The water scorpion's body looked like a slender twig stuck among the Elodea leaves. Like Anax, it usually stayed still and waited for its food to come to it. The water scorpion's front legs stretched out in front of its body, ready to seize an insect. It watched Anax as he clung to a plant just a few inches away, resting from the ordeal of shedding his old exoskeleton. Minutes passed; he did not see the water scorpion.

Anax was motionless except for the slight rhythmic movement of his abdomen as he pumped water in and out. Strong muscles caused water to rush into his anus and flow over simple gills within his rectum. The gills took oxygen from water. This is how Anax breathed.

The water scorpion had no underwater breathing apparatus. Eventually it needed to replenish its oxygen supply. It swam up to the surface, then thrust its long rear breathing tube up into the air.

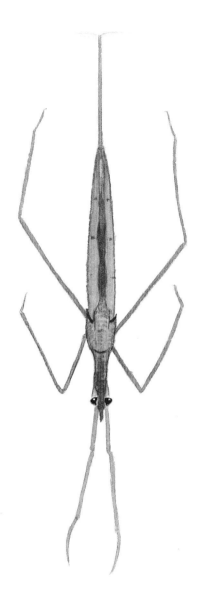

A water scorpion is not a scorpion. It is an insect, a true bug, related to the giant water bug, back swimmer, water boatman, and water strider.

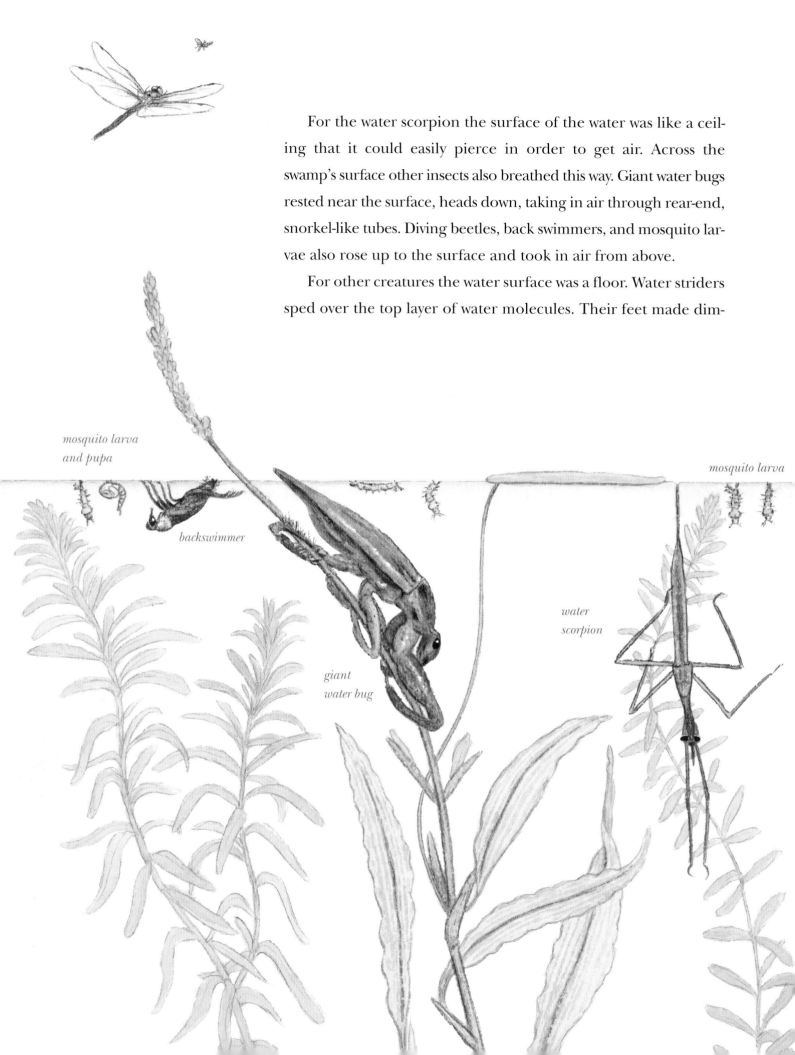

For the water scorpion the surface of the water was like a ceiling that it could easily pierce in order to get air. Across the swamp's surface other insects also breathed this way. Giant water bugs rested near the surface, heads down, taking in air through rear-end, snorkel-like tubes. Diving beetles, back swimmers, and mosquito larvae also rose up to the surface and took in air from above.

For other creatures the water surface was a floor. Water striders sped over the top layer of water molecules. Their feet made dim-

mosquito larva and pupa

mosquito larva

backswimmer

water scorpion

giant water bug

ples in the water, but pads of waxy hairs on their feet helped keep them from plunging through. Near shore, fishing spiders dashed over the surface. Bigger and heavier than water striders, they still did not break the surface layer of water molecules. Thousands of hairs on their legs and bodies help spread their weight over a wide area.

All of this went unseen by Anax, whose vision was not yet fully developed. However, each time he molted and emerged with a larger

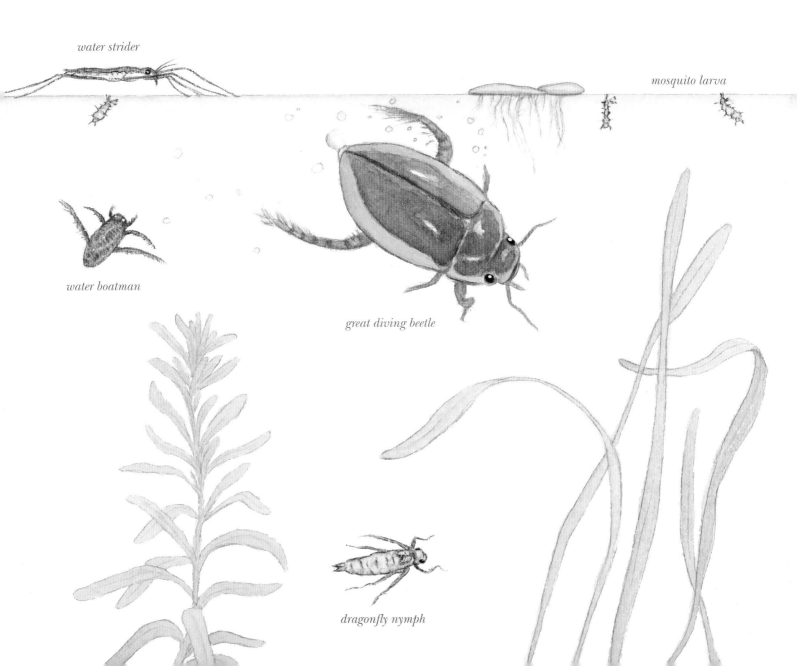

water strider

mosquito larva

water boatman

great diving beetle

dragonfly nymph

exoskeleton, his eyes took up a bigger area of his face. His vision grew sharper. It was especially good at detecting motion—useful both for catching food and for not being caught as food.

One June morning his eyesight would help save his life. Anax spotted a mosquito larva that had settled upon some waterweed leaves. Step-by-step he stalked it. Just a few more steps and the larva would be his.

Then Anax saw motion above—a big, dark shape hurtling toward him. The muscles in his abdomen contracted swiftly, forcing a jet of water out behind him. The force pushed Anax in the opposite direction. He jetted away through the water. His legs were pressed against his abdomen, giving him a more stream-lined shape. In a second he darted nearly half a foot.

As Anax slowed, the muscles in his abdomen relaxed. Water rushed into his rear. Then, in an instant, the muscles tightened and the water spurted out. Anax jetted away again. In a series of spurts, he zoomed several feet to safety.

The dark shape that had hurtled toward Anax was a giant water bug, a fierce underwater predator. It stopped chasing him when it spied a damselfly nymph just an inch away. The water bug lunged and seized the nymph with its powerful front legs. It pulled the struggling nymph close and pierced its abdomen with its beak, injecting chemicals called enzymes that turned the nymph's innards into fluid.

As the giant water bug began to sip its meal, Anax rested a safe distance away on the stem of an arrowhead plant. It was late June. Anax had survived for a month as a nymph. He had molted four times and was now about a half inch long. In his escape from his pursuer, Anax had entered into new and unfamiliar underwater territory. Further adventures lay ahead.

Giant water bugs are ferocious predators. They sometimes attack fish, frogs, and tadpoles several times their size. Their mouthparts pierce prey and suck fluids from them. A warning to barefoot pond explorers: giant water bugs are also called "toe biters!"

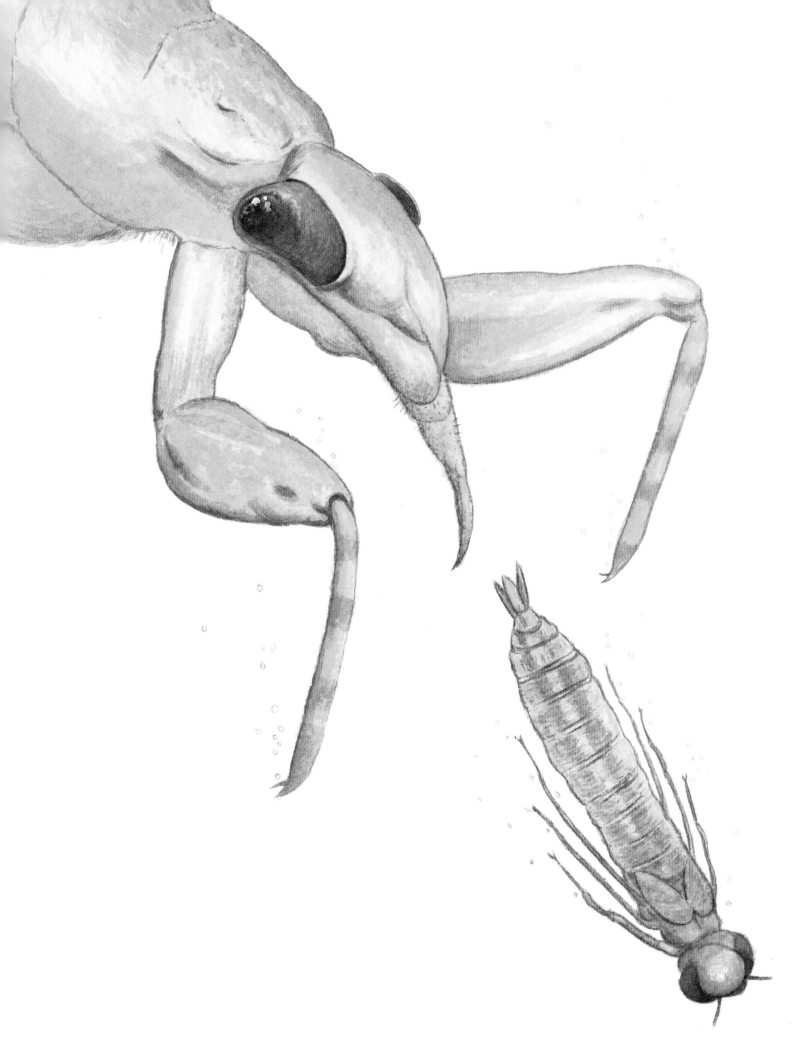

A Life of Peril and a New Beginning

*O*N A mid-July morning the swamp smelled of mint. Spearmint grew abundantly along one shore, and deer had crushed some leaves as they drank at dawn, releasing the tangy scent. The seed heads of cattail plants were turning brown. Swamp milkweed and boneset were in bloom, and cardinal flowers blazed from little hummocks of land that were scattered throughout the swamp.

Damselflies flitted among the shore plants, catching midges and gnats. A female red-waisted whiteface flew low over the water. She dipped her abdomen into the water again and again, releasing eggs that sank into the thickets of waterweeds.

A great blue heron stood absolutely still, waiting and watching. Then, with one swift stab it seized a tadpole and swallowed it. The splash and commotion sent other creatures scurrying. The heron bent its head down close to the water, looking around intently. A dragonfly nymph jetted right into view.

Splash! The heron swallowed a green darner nymph. It was a large, fully grown nymph, nearly two inches long. However, it was not one of Anax's sisters or brothers. It was from another green

Female dragonflies and damselflies are very choosy about where they lay their eggs. Some species deposit eggs only in swift-flowing water, even in waterfalls. Others must have the still water of ponds. A particular kind of habitat is necessary for the nymphs to survive and develop into adults.

In 1971 a Canadian scientist, Robert Trottier, reported finding two populations of green darners: year-round residents and migrators. Other observers have since confirmed his discovery. The two populations probably do not inter-breed because the migrators mate in the spring and early summer, the residents in mid-to-late summer.

The nymphs of dragonflies and damselflies are sensitive to water pollution. The presence—or absence—of certain species of nymphs is a vital clue to the health of a river or lake. If water is too polluted for most nymphs, it is also unhealthy for crayfish, mussels, and other freshwater life. The state of Florida, among others, has begun to use dragonfly and damselfly nymphs as "pollution indicator species" for lakes and streams.

darner population. Scientists have found two groups of green darners in northern parts of the United States and in southern Canada. These darner populations seem exactly alike except for one remarkable difference.

One population of green darners lives year-round in the north. The nymphs spend the winter in ponds and other wetlands. They grow to be adults that mate and leave a new generation of nymphs in the north. This population does not migrate. The other green darner population flies north in the spring and mates there. These new nymphs develop through the summer and become adults that fly south in the fall and mate there. The nymph named Anax was part of this population of green darners.

Anax had made narrow escapes from green darner nymphs of the year-round population. They were twice his size—top predators that often ate smaller dragonfly and damselfly nymphs. But the large nymphs themselves made tasty morsels for frogs and for herons patrolling the water's edge.

A pair of wood ducks frequently paddled through the swamp. Mostly they ate tiny floating duckweeds, but sometimes they probed the Elodea with their bills, catching dragonfly nymphs. But they did not catch Anax.

On sunny days, when the water near the surface grew uncomfortably warm, Anax moved deeper among the waterweeds. And at night he sometimes crept down to the bottom and hunted there. His keen eyesight was of little use in the dark, but short antennae on his head and touch sensors on his body detected movements in the surrounding water. Anax caught snails and small tadpoles in the bottom mud.

At daybreak Anax would be back near the surface, resting on

damselfly gills

The gills of a dragonfly nymph
are hidden inside its abdomen,
while gills of a damselfly are outside.
They look like three feathers at the
tip of its abdomen.

Elodea leaves, alert for more food. He seldom had to go far.
The waterweeds were rich with life: small beetles and bugs, back
swimmers, mosquito larvae, and nymphs of both dragonflies
and damselflies.

A damselfly nymph crept into view. Anax waited for it to
come closer. Slowly he turned his head and trained his large
eyes on the damselfly. As the nymph moved toward him, Anax's
brain judged the distance between them.

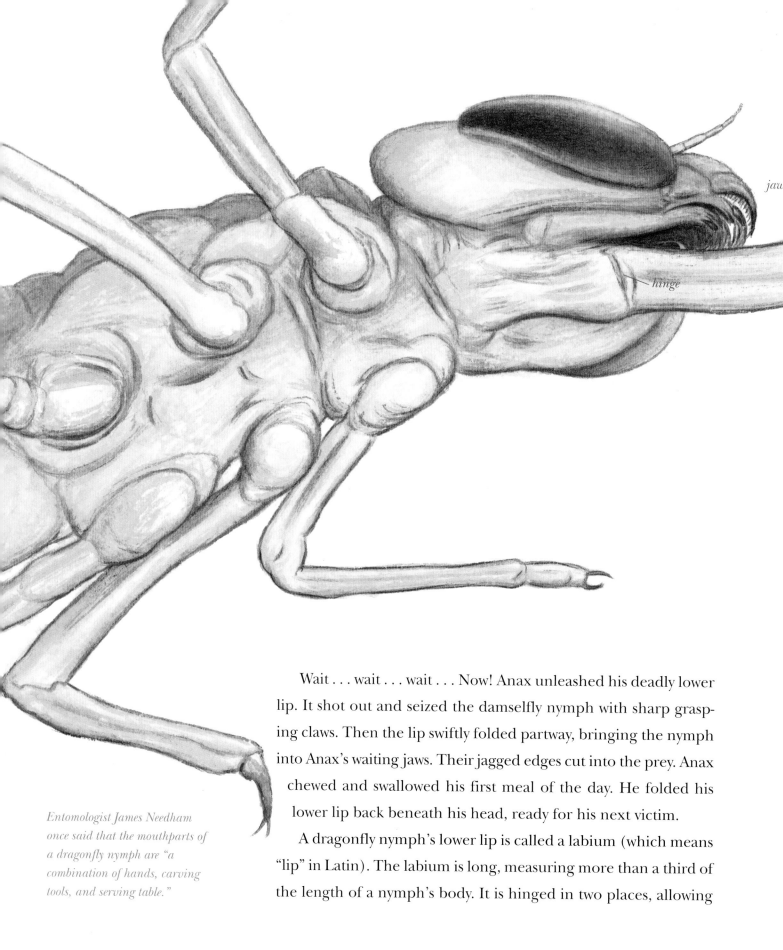

jaws

hinge

Entomologist James Needham once said that the mouthparts of a dragonfly nymph are "a combination of hands, carving tools, and serving table."

Wait . . . wait . . . wait . . . Now! Anax unleashed his deadly lower lip. It shot out and seized the damselfly nymph with sharp grasping claws. Then the lip swiftly folded partway, bringing the nymph into Anax's waiting jaws. Their jagged edges cut into the prey. Anax chewed and swallowed his first meal of the day. He folded his lower lip back beneath his head, ready for his next victim.

A dragonfly nymph's lower lip is called a labium (which means "lip" in Latin). The labium is long, measuring more than a third of the length of a nymph's body. It is hinged in two places, allowing

26

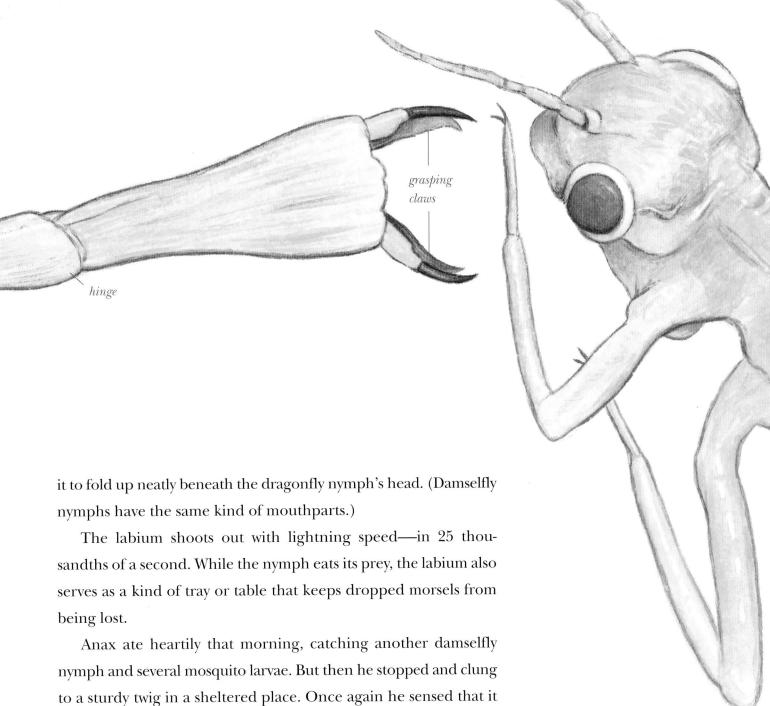

hinge

grasping claws

it to fold up neatly beneath the dragonfly nymph's head. (Damselfly nymphs have the same kind of mouthparts.)

The labium shoots out with lightning speed—in 25 thousandths of a second. While the nymph eats its prey, the labium also serves as a kind of tray or table that keeps dropped morsels from being lost.

Anax ate heartily that morning, catching another damselfly nymph and several mosquito larvae. But then he stopped and clung to a sturdy twig in a sheltered place. Once again he sensed that it was time to grow, time for a new, bigger exoskeleton. Within a day Anax had molted.

With each molt Anax not only grew in size but changed in other ways. His eyes in particular grew larger. Wing buds appeared on the back of his thorax. They too grew larger with each molt. If Anax survived to be an adult, these wing buds would develop into the extraordinary wings that would carry Anax swiftly through the air.

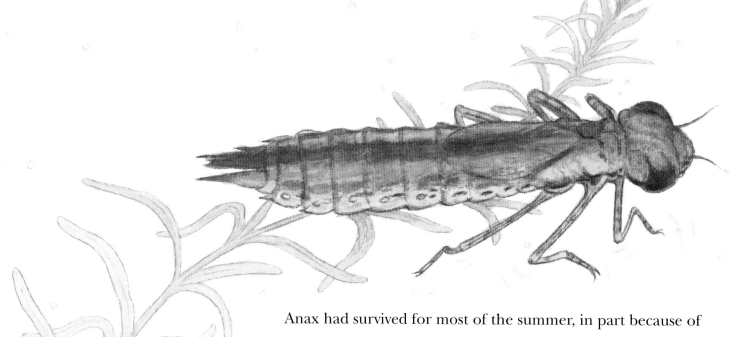

Anax had survived for most of the summer, in part because of luck. He was lucky that there were no fish in the swamp. Although a good-sized dragonfly nymph can catch and eat small fish, larger fish often prey on nymphs. The nymphs of some kinds of damselflies and dragonflies lurk on the bottom, hidden in mud and decaying leaves; fish often overlook them. Green darner nymphs, however, spend most of their lives off the bottom, on cattails and other water plants, where perch, bass, and other predatory fish may find them.

Even without fish, life in the swamp had been a gauntlet of predators for Anax and the nymphs that had hatched from his mother's eggs. Only a few had survived. But now, late in the summer, the survivors themselves had become big enough to be among the top underwater predators in the swamp.

In early September, Anax molted one last time as a nymph. His new exoskeleton was nearly two inches long. He could now catch and eat bigger prey—bigger tadpoles, beetles, and nymphs. He was a powerful force in his part of the swamp. One day an Eastern newt swam close to Anax and eyed him. The salamander was three inches long. It would have eaten Anax when he was a young nymph. For a few moments Anax and the newt stared at each other. Then the newt swam off.

Anax was still vulnerable to large predators, so he stayed alert.

In his final nymph form, his eyes continued to grow until they covered the whole upper surface of his head. This gave him exceptional vision for spotting prey and avoiding enemies. One day Anax saw a huge, dark shape loom overhead, above the water, and jetted toward a hideout in the waterweeds. With a great splash, a kingfisher dove into the water. An instant later the kingfisher beat its powerful wings and rose out again. Its beak held only a strand of Elodea. Anax had escaped.

Although flowers still bloomed along the swamp's shore, there were signs that summer was ending. The mating songs of birds were stilled. Red maple leaves showed hints of the brilliant scarlet to come.

Anax continued to feast on the swamp's smorgasbord, but something caused him to change his behavior. Perhaps it was the days growing shorter, or the water growing cooler, or something within Anax himself. He ate less and moved toward shore, resting among some cattails.

A female forktail damselfly backed down a cattail leaf in front of him. She had landed above water and began laying eggs in the leaf near the surface. The damselfly continued to descend down the leaf, laying more eggs. She was a foot underwater when she died in Anax's jaws.

The damselfly was Anax's last meal underwater. He stopped eating entirely, a remarkable change for such an ever-hungry creature. He also breathed more rapidly than ever before, taking in as much oxygen as possible. Anax became more active at night than during the day. He explored along the water's edge. He touched twigs and the stems of cattail flowers—testing them, sensing whether they provided a firm gripping surface. One night Anax crept up a cattail stem until his body was out of the water partway. He felt air for the first time and breathed some in through little openings in his thorax. Before dawn he retreated underwater and rested all day long.

When the world grew dark, Anax crept up the cattail stem once more. This time his whole body broke clear of the water. Anax kept climbing, leaving behind his watery home forever. As he climbed he tested the surface with his claws.

At last he found a place that seemed just right. He dug his claws into the stem's fibers. He swung his abdomen from side to side several times. Then he grew still.

Some of Anax's brothers and sisters had also crept out of the water in the dark, along the swamp's shore and by hummocks out in the water. The darkness was vital. In a life full of danger this was perhaps the most dangerous time of all for the nymphs. They were utterly helpless, now easy prey for blackbirds, herons, and other birds. But the birds were asleep. The green darner nymphs had a few hours to undergo one last molt, one last shedding of their exoskeletons.

Anax was motionless except for a pumping motion in his abdomen. He swallowed air, and as the air pressure increased, his thorax and head began to bulge. At last they split open. Anax in his new form began to appear. First his head, thorax, and some of his new legs emerged. Gradually he freed the rest of his legs.

Anax's back was arched and he hung upside down in the air, held only by his abdomen, which was still inside his nymph exoskeleton. He hung that way for several minutes, resting. After a while his new legs hardened. Now he was ready for the final and hardest part of his emergence as a young adult green darner.

Anax suddenly jerked upward and groped around in the dark with his feet. He grabbed hold of the front of his nymph skin. He squirmed and wriggled and pulled his abdomen out of the back of the tight-fitting nymph exoskeleton. Now he was completely free.

At first Anax looked bedraggled and misshapen. His abdomen was bent in a sort of half-moon shape, its segments scrunched together. His wings were small, soft, and crumpled. Anax began pumping blood and air into his wings, thorax, and abdomen. They slowly began to inflate like a balloon. His abdomen segments

Why do nymphs usually wiggle their abdomens before changing into adults? One possibility is to make sure there's a clear space on both sides for the new adult to spread its wings. Another possibility is the nymph is checking its grip on the surface. A firm grip is vital. If a half-emerged dragonfly falls, it is helpless and dies. A sudden wind-storm can cause the death of many emerging dragonflies.

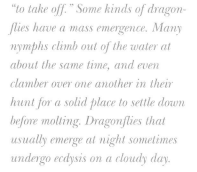

expanded like a telescope. Blood flowed into a network of veins in his wings. The wings began to unfold and expand. He crawled up the stem a few inches.

One half hour later, Anax was twice as long as the hollow nymph exoskeleton that still clung to the cattail stem a few inches away. His wings were full size. At first he held them together over his back, then flicked them out to the sides. Each of his four wings stretched out at right angles to his thorax, giving him a wingspan of five inches.

Even though Anax was now full size, his body and wings were still soft and easily damaged. He remained still for the rest of the night. Gradually, the cuticle of his new exoskeleton grew harder and darker. The veins in his wings also began to harden. In a few hours, Anax had changed from a creature that crept and sometimes jetted about underwater to one that would soon swoop through the air.

Darkness began to fade. A new day was coming, and with it the dawn of a new life for Anax.

A Living Flash of Light

*T*HERE was an autumn chill in the morning air. The temperature within Anax's body was too low for flight, but the dragonfly wisdom stored in his brain told him to fly away from the swamp as soon as possible.

From the moment Anax emerged from his egg his life had been full of peril. This morning was no exception. A flock of migrating grackles had roosted overnight in nearby trees. Now the air was full of their clattering calls as they awoke and began to fly down to hunt for food along the swamp edge.

Still clinging tightly to the cattail stem, Anax began to vibrate his wings. They made a slight whirring sound. He fluttered them rapidly, minute after minute. Gradually the burning of energy warmed his body, and the temperature rose within his thorax. Soon Anax would be able to fly.

Some of his brothers and sisters were not so lucky. They too had emerged as dragonflies in the night, but had started later. When morning came, their wings were not yet ready for flight. Immobile and helpless, several green darners were easy prey for the grackles.

Today I saw the dragon-fly
Come from the wells where he did lie.
An inner impulse rent the veil
Of his old husk; from head to tail
Came out clear plates of sapphire mail.
He dried his wings: like gauze they grew;
Thro' crofts and pastures wet with dew
A living flash of light he flew.

—from "The Two Voices"
by Alfred Lord Tennyson

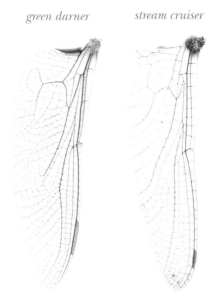

At first glance a dragonfly wing may look like a confusing mess of crisscrossing lines, but there is a pattern to the arrangement of veins. The different species have distinct vein patterns. Entomologists use the patterns to help identify dragonfly species.

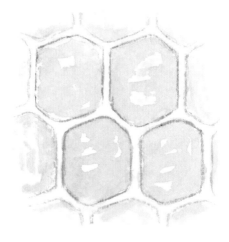

Almost all insects have compound eyes, made up of many facets. On the surface of the eye, each facet is shaped like a hexagon. Houseflies have about four thousand facets in each eye; a green darner has seven times as many. This magnified view of a dragonfly eye shows some of its six-sided facets.

The birds plucked off the untried wings, then ate the dragonfly bodies.

Still beating his wings, Anax loosened his tight grip on the cattail stem. He rose into the air and over the forest that surrounded the wetland, then swooped low to land in a bush. Ahead lay a grassy field studded with blooming goldenrod and aster. Bees, flies, and a wealth of other flying insects moved among the flowers. Anax rested for a moment before beginning to hunt.

The hollow veins in his four wings that had carried blood and air had hardened. The intricate network of rigid veins gives dragonflies the strongest wings of all large insects. Anax himself, however, was not strong.

A newly emerged dragonfly is a pale imitation of the swift predator it will become. Anax was not yet able to mate and reproduce. More important, his new body was a sort of hollow shell. His flight muscles were not yet fully developed, and he had almost no fat reserves for energy. He was in what scientists call his teneral stage. (*Teneral* comes from a Latin word that means "tender" or "delicate.") When Anax flew over the forest to the edge of the field, his flight had been slow and fluttery, more like that of a damselfly than a dragonfly. Anax rested, scarcely moving. His abdomen swelled slightly and lowered. Then it narrowed slightly and raised. This rhythm continued as Anax inhaled and exhaled air through tiny openings in his thorax and abdomen called spiracles. Tubes within his abdomen and thorax carried oxygen to all parts of his body.

Anax also moved his head a bit. His neck was short and tiny, but very flexible. He could pivot his head from side to side, and up and down, another remarkable dragonfly characteristic. Most insects cannot move their heads at all. They must move their entire bodies in order to look in another direction.

With just slight head movements Anax could see all around, including above and behind him. Each of his bulging, wrap-around eyes contained more than twenty-eight thousand facets. Each facet had its own lens and nerve connection to Anax's brain. The facets on the upper part of Anax's eyes were bigger than those on the lower part. The bigger facets were best at sensing movement and spotting prey in the air. The smaller facets were best at seeing an insect perched on a flower or other objects below.

As Anax looked over the field, he could see bees and other insects flying as far as sixty feet away. He needed food. He launched into the air and went after his first meal as an adult dragonfly.

He flew slowly, but fast enough to overtake a mosquito. He caught it in the basketlike trap formed by his spiny legs, then brought it up to his mouth. He held the mosquito with his lower lip and quickly chopped it up with his mandibles (jaws). Anax did not land to eat. Instead, he hovered in the air, swallowed the mosquito, then flew off in search of more prey.

Just ahead, a honeybee rose from some goldenrod blossoms. It flew slowly, its legs loaded with pollen. In an instant Anax closed in and caught the bee. He landed on an aster bough to eat it. Afterward he cleaned up. Like a cat grooming himself after a meal, Anax swept bits of food from his eyes and antennae with comblike barbs on his front legs. Then he cleaned the combs with his mouth.

Anax rose above the flowers, paused, turned, and looked about. A medium-sized dragonfly—a clubtail—flew into view. Anax flew toward it, but the clubtail easily sped out of sight. Anax was still no match for fast-flying insects.

He spied a small insect take flight below him. A ladybird beetle flew slowly among the stems and flowers of goldenrods and asters. Anax chased after it down a twisting passageway among the plants.

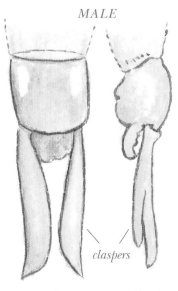

MALE

claspers

top view   side view

In the 1700s an Englishman named John Abbott collected insects in North America and made drawings of them. He collected the very first specimens of several species. His notes report handling a dragonfly "when I was told it wou'd sting as bad as a Rattle Snake bite." Dragonflies have no stingers. Males have two claspers at the end of their abdomens that enable them to hold on to a female when mating or flying in tandem. Females have an ovipositor, or egg-laying device, which contains two pairs of sharp blades at the end of their abdomens. These are used to cut slits in leaves, into which eggs are then laid.

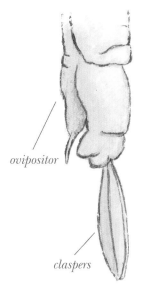

FEMALE

ovipositor

claspers   side view

Rounding a corner, the beetle flew right through an open space in a spiderweb stretched across the alleyway. But Anax saw the web too late and slammed into several sticky strands.

A large spider, a black-and-yellow Argiope, felt the impact. It had already caught and killed a grasshopper and a damselfly; their bodies were partly wrapped in silken thread. The spider stepped toward Anax.

The strands of spider silk were strong—but not strong enough to hold a green darner, even one in its weak teneral stage. Anax twisted and turned. He beat his wings. He broke free and flew to the top of a tree at the edge of the field. The spider began to repair its damaged web. Anax groomed himself, wiping bits of spider silk from his eyes.

As cool twilight crept over the field, the mosquitoes became more active. Anax easily caught and ate a dozen, then flew to the top of a tree. Anax had survived his first day in his teneral stage. He had eaten well and grown stronger. It was time for a much-needed rest.

Argiopes are large spiders that often wait for prey by hanging head down at the center of their wheel-shaped orb webs. The black-and-yellow Argiope is sometimes called the "golden garden spider."

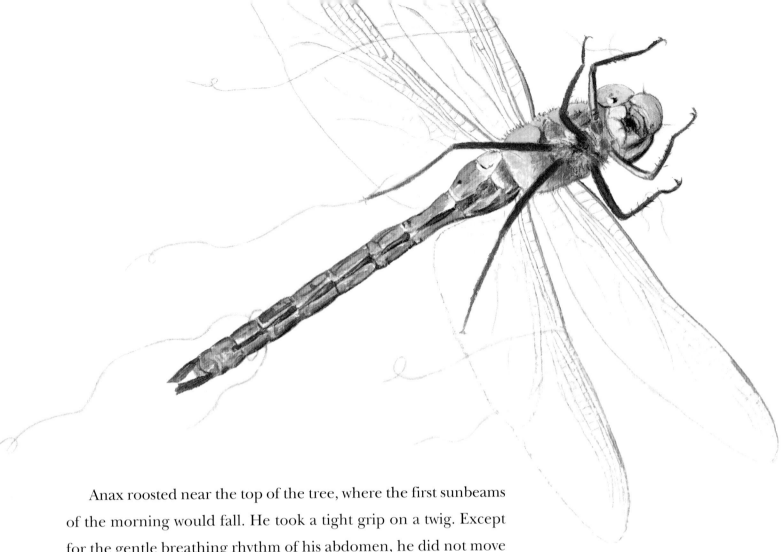

Anax roosted near the top of the tree, where the first sunbeams of the morning would fall. He took a tight grip on a twig. Except for the gentle breathing rhythm of his abdomen, he did not move until dawn.

For the next few days Anax's life settled into a routine. He awoke early and began whirring his wings to warm his flight muscles. Then the hunt for food began. Usually he ate on the wing, landing only to chew up a big catch. In the fading light he flew to a tree and settled down for the night. One day he stayed in his tree, clinging to a twig, as rain pelted the leaves above. Dragonflies rarely fly in the rain.

Anax did, however, occasionally need water to drink. Hovering just above the water's surface, he sipped from ponds and, one day, from a slow-flowing stretch of French Creek—a few miles from the swamp where he had spent his nymph life. He was free to roam the countryside and hunted wherever he came upon flying insects to eat. He patrolled the air space above a flock of sheep—flies some-

Each year the last thing that billions of mosquitoes see is the face of a dragonfly. Dragonflies catch and eat so many mosquitoes that they are sometimes called "mosquito hawks." At Isle Royale National Park in Lake Superior, park workers look forward to the spring emergence of "the Isle Royale Air Force"—the dragonflies. They feast on the black flies, deer flies, and mosquitoes that swarm around people; they will even pluck these insects right off a person's skin!

times flew up from the sheep's woolly coats. As the sheep grazed, grasshoppers, small moths, and other insects flew or leaped into the air. Anax zoomed down again and again to catch them.

One windless, humid afternoon Anax flew near a vegetable garden and saw many small, slow-flying insects rising into the air. The insects were flying ants. Young queens and thousands of males were emerging from nests by a stone wall. A few of the queens would mate and dig into the soil, where new ant colonies would develop. Most of the unmated queens and all of the males would soon die. And this day, many died soon after emerging from the soil, as a house wren, a flicker, barn swallows, and several different dragonflies flew in to take advantage of the wealth of food.

Anax, along with a black saddlebags and a white-tailed skimmer, feasted on the ants. Anax and the saddlebags ate most of the ants where they caught them—in the air. The white-tailed skimmer, however, would rest on top of a fence post, dash out to catch a flying ant, then return to perch on the post while eating. All dragonflies can be divided into these two ways of hunting: perchers or fliers. All darners, including green darners, are fliers.

Early in his teneral stage Anax had rested often. He simply

white-tailed skimmer

green darner

wasn't strong enough to keep flying. But as the days passed, his vora-
cious feeding gave him fat reserves for energy. His flight muscles
grew stronger, and he was able to chase and catch faster prey. Soon
he would be able to fly with all of the speed, grace, and agility of a
mature dragonfly.

His wings were strong but flexible. They could not only beat up
and down but also twist and bend. They were powered in a way
unique among insects. Most flying insects have four wings that all
move together as a unit. Dragonflies and damselflies also have four
wings, but the front and back pairs move independently. Each wing
has its own set of eight muscles. As a result, the front pair of wings
can move downward while the back pair is on the upbeat. This creates a swirl of air called a vortex. Airplanes and birds have trouble
with an unsteady flow of air over their wings, but dragonflies take
advantage of turbulent air—it actually helps keep them aloft.

Fine hairs on the upper surface of Anax's wings measured the airflow. His eyes kept track of his surroundings, including the horizon. All of this information was sent to his brain. Without thinking, Anax made dozens of changes in his wing and body positions every minute. He stayed parallel to the ground or water below, and made split-second maneuvers in the air.

Anax could hover in midair, then beat all four wings together and, in a few seconds, accelerate to thirty miles per hour. He could dart to the side, fly backward for a short distance, and even turn an aerial somersault. Flying swiftly, he could stop in an instant by lowering his abdomen and hind legs.

Anax beat his wings no more than thirty times per second. This was slow compared with bees or flies that beat their wings two to three hundred times per second, but the number of wing beats did not matter—Anax could still catch those bees and flies. As he continued to kill and eat, his flight muscles grew. Eventually these muscles would make up nearly half of his weight.

Dragonflies are believed to navigate by observing the position of the sun in the sky (called sun compass navigation). An internal "clock" automatically compensates for the earth's rotation and helps keep the dragonfly on course.

For several days Anax wandered the Sherman, New York, area. Now he sensed it was time for a change. He was not yet a fully developed green darner in strength or in color, but he was ready to begin migration. One morning in late September, Anax ate several mosquitoes and a robber fly. He landed briefly and cleaned his eyes. Then he lifted into the air and began to fly south.

Near the ground he felt a light breeze blowing from the northwest. But higher in the air, clear of trees, the breeze felt stronger. At first Anax flew at treetop level. Gradually he rose higher, then higher still. The more altitude he gained, the stronger the air moved toward the southeast. It carried Anax along. Sometimes he beat his wings, sometimes he just glided without effort.

Below lay a landscape of farms and forests. Within minutes Anax passed from New York into Pennsylvania. The rural landscape, with scattered small towns, stayed the same. Anax flew on, taking advantage of the extra push from the wind.

He was not alone in the sky. A flock of tree swallows kept pace with Anax for a while, then descended toward a lake that gleamed below like a silver jewel. Occasionally other dragonflies appeared—green darners and black saddlebags. A blue dasher flew near Anax. The two dragonflies veered away from each other.

Smaller flying insects and even tiny spiders, carried aloft by their lines of silk, sometimes appeared near Anax. He fed as he flew. The in-flight meals allowed him to keep flying for several hours. Only as daylight faded did Anax glide down to roost in a sugar maple tree. Its leaves were just beginning to change from summer green to autumn gold.

Anax made little progress in the next two days. He ate almost nothing as rain pelted down, day and night. Then, at last, a cold front began to move in. Sunlight broke through the clouds. The late-afternoon sun backlit hordes of gnats, midges, crane flies, and other insects that looked to be dancing in the air over a meadow. Dragonflies flew back and forth in a feeding swarm. They were all famished.

Dragonflies seem to disappear on cloudy days. They are creatures of the sun. On this afternoon it seemed especially true. As Anax darted, hovered, and dived, his wings shimmered in the sunlight. He was truly "a living flash of light."

No people were around to admire the beauty of the dragonfly-feeding swarm, but a kestrel watched from its perch on a telephone line. Kestrels are sometimes called "sparrow hawks" in North America, but they eat many more grasshoppers and other large insects than sparrows. They also eat dragonflies.

The black saddlebags was formerly called the "black-mantled glider." It has a black blotch at the base of each hind wing. From a distance these marks make the dragonfly's body appear bulky, as though it were carrying saddlebags like a horse. It is the second most commonly observed migratory dragonfly in North America, after the green darner.

merlin

Mississippi kite

Hawks called merlins and hawklike birds called Mississippi kites also catch dragonflies. Despite their excellent vision, dragonflies have a blind spot to the rear and below. Hawks that swoop underneath dragonflies from the rear are able to catch dozens in a day. Green darners seem to be an important food source for migrating merlins and kestrels.

The kestrel lifted off the telephone line and flew parallel to the meadow, gaining altitude. Then it swung out over the meadow, above the dragonflies, looking for a target. He spotted one—a big dragonfly moving slowly, feasting among a cloud of gnats. It was Anax.

The kestrel flew closer but stayed behind and well above Anax. A kestrel's vision is much sharper than any insect's eyesight, even that of a dragonfly's. It hovered for a moment, then tipped forward, closing its wings tightly against its body and falling like a spear pointed at Anax.

As the kestrel dove it could see Anax in fine detail. Anax was watching some gnats a few feet ahead of him. But his huge wrap-around eyes quickly detected other movement. Anax darted to the right. He felt a rush of air as the kestrel zoomed past.

The kestrel opened its wings, breaking its free fall, then turned back toward Anax. This time it tried direct pursuit, chasing Anax around the meadow. Anax darted left and right, outmaneuvering the bird. It gave up. The kestrel spotted another dragonfly in slow, fluttery flight. It was a green darner that was in its early teneral stage. The kestrel sped toward it. In an instant the darner was in the kestrel's beak. Like silvery autumn leaves, four dragonfly wings sailed slowly down to nestle in the grass.

Kestrels are about the size of a robin, but with a longer tail. They often hover in the air as they pinpoint the location of a mouse or large insect below. They nest in hollow trees or in birdhouses. Sometimes dragonfly wings are found in or beneath the nest—evidence that the adult kestrels feed dragonflies to their young.

By dawn the next day, Anax was speeding southeast, sometimes due east, as a passenger in a fast-moving mass of air. In calm air he would have flown straight south, but he took advantage of the wind; this way he could travel fast without using much energy but still gain ground toward the south. The numbers of dragonflies around him grew. So did the numbers of migrating birds, and of monarch butterflies. Some of the monarchs had emerged as adults in Pennsylvania and had just begun their journey to central Mexico.

Two days of northwest winds helped carry Anax to eastern Pennsylvania. He felt an updraft of air as he flew near the north lookout of Hawk Mountain Sanctuary. The rising air lifted Anax near a cluster of people on the rocky lookout point. They were watching the hawk migration, keeping a tally of sixteen hawk and eagle species that pass by Hawk Mountain each fall. This late September day had brought sightings of more than two hundred sharp-shinned hawks and nearly fifty broad-winged hawks. And, some of the watchers noted, it also brought scores of migrating dragonflies, mostly green darners.

Northwest winds continued to push the migrants along. When

Anax settled down in a treetop for the night he was in southern New Jersey. The next day Anax awoke to calm, warm air. He had flown southward far enough to reach a warmer climate than the place where his life began, in western New York. He no longer needed wing-whirring to warm his flight muscles in the morning.

Today there was no wind pushing Anax eastward. He flew south, pausing over a soccer field, and later a pasture, to catch food. Still, Anax passed over many miles of land, flying deeper and deeper into southern New Jersey. The migrants around him grew more abundant.

Anax saw more dragonflies, more monarch butterflies, and more hawks. None of the fliers knew that they were all flying into a sort of funnel: the narrowing peninsula at the southernmost tip of New Jersey.

Anax arrived in Cape May, New Jersey, in early October. Sunlight gleamed off the Atlantic Ocean to the east and Delaware Bay to the south and west. Anax flew away from the shore and perched in a tree. He had crossed rivers and small lakes but never a large body of water. He sensed danger ahead.

Each summer the last generation of monarch butterflies west of the Rocky Mountains flies to wintering roosts on the California coast. East of the Rockies, late summer monarchs try to reach mountainous forest refuges west of Mexico City.

A Dragon in the Sky

MIGRATORY birds usually do not pause for long at the southernmost tip of New Jersey. They cross nearly fifteen miles of Delaware Bay and continue their flight south. Monarch butterflies also fly directly across, but sometimes wait several days for favorable wind conditions. Dragonflies seem even more cautious. Although they have been seen over large bodies of water, there are also reports of dragonflies flying around such waters, including Lake Ontario and other Great Lakes. Dragonflies can be pushed off course by strong winds. At Cape May a powerful wind from the west or northwest could force them far out over the ocean.

Fortunately for the dragonflies, there was a light northwest wind on this early October day. People who had gathered at the hawk-watch platform at Cape May Point State Park noticed a steady stream of dragonflies arriving from the north. All along the southern shore dragonflies patrolled the air above the dunes. They were mostly black saddlebags. A short distance inland, above the fields at Higbee Beach Wildlife Management Area, the air was filled with green darners.

Cape May, New Jersey, is one of the best places in the entire United States to witness the fall migration of hawks, monarch butterflies, and dragonflies. On more than one occasion, many dragonflies have been seen flying north from Cape May, apparently to avoid crossing Delaware Bay at its widest part. During one hour and a half period on September 11, 1992, an estimated four hundred thousand dragonflies, mostly green darners, flew over Cape May and then northward.

black saddlebags

green darner

swamp darner

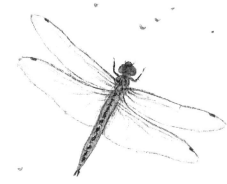

wandering glider

The wandering glider is well named; it is an extraordinary traveler. This dragonfly lives all over the world except for Europe, Antarctica, and the Arctic. Large numbers once landed on a ship more than eight hundred miles from the coast of Australia, from which they had probably flown. This species and other gliders all have broad-based hind wings that enable them to glide easily and travel far while using little energy.

spot-winged glider

They swooped, hovered, turned, and sped above the fields. For every darner hunting in the air, there were many more resting in trees or near the ground, clinging to asters, ragweed, or goldenrod. Anax was among them. He waited, conserving his energy. All of the dragonflies seemed to be waiting for something.

On the next day the northwest breeze continued; in fact, it grew stronger. This seemed to be a signal. The dragonflies began flying. They did not set out over the open water of Delaware Bay. Instead they flew *north*, into the wind. They stayed low, within fifty feet of the ground, and flew along the eastern shore of Delaware Bay. They flew steadily and swiftly, leaving Cape May far behind. Then, in midafternoon, thousands of dragonflies turned and flew west over Delaware Bay. They crossed where the water is only about four miles wide.

Anax rested in Delaware that night, holding onto a branch of a black cherry tree. The next morning, after catching some flies and small moths, he began flying south. Countless other dragonflies were also on the move. They moved through the air with fluid grace. They were a flowing river of dragonflies.

Mixed among the green darners were several other species. There were black saddlebags, Carolina saddlebags, spot-winged

Carolina saddlebags

twelve-spotted skimmer

gliders, and wandering gliders. There were also twelve-spotted skimmers, swamp darners, and blue dashers. The largest numbers by far were green darners.

Five days after crossing Delaware Bay, Anax reached the southern tip of Virginia's Delmarva Peninsula. Fisherman's Island lay just offshore. Beyond the island stretched more than seventeen miles of water at the mouth of Chesapeake Bay. No land was in sight at the horizon, but a slender thread of roadway and bridges did lead across the water—the Chesapeake Bay Bridge Tunnel. Anax did not hesitate. He flew steadily along this safe path across the water and reached land near Norfolk in less than an hour.

As they migrated, Anax and other dragonflies sometimes flew at a steady twenty-five miles per hour. At that pace, flying from dawn until dusk, they could cover three hundred miles in a day. They paused many times, however, to feed in swarms over farm fields, marshes, and any other open space where flying insects were plentiful. On cloudy and rainy days, the dragonflies rested. Sometimes hundreds of dragonflies hung beneath the leaves of a single tree. They often roosted close to the ground in a field or in shrubs.

At night the faint calls of migrating songbirds wafted down to dragonflies at rest. In the daytime Anax saw other kinds of songbirds,

Whether they migrate or not, dragonflies often gather early or late in the day and feed in a swarm. Four or more species may be attracted to places where midges, gnats, crane flies, and mosquitoes are abundant in the air. Dragonfly swarm feeding was first illustrated in the thirteenth century by a Chinese artist in a scroll painting called "Early Autumn."

blue dasher

Dragonflies are admired and honored in many cultures. To the Hopi and Zuni people they are a symbol of hope and good luck in the deserts of the American Southwest. They are rain messengers in an arid land. A Zuni myth tells how a boy created the very first dragonfly. He tried to make a butterfly for his little sister, but the creature he made from a piece of cornstalk, straws, and paint was unlike any insect ever seen. It came to life and brought rain and food to the Zuni.

as well as migrating hawks. Along the seashore he twice dodged and dived to escape being eaten by terns. And one day, flying a quarter mile in the air above the Cape Fear River in North Carolina, he saw a merlin clutch a nearby green darner in its talons. It nipped off the dragonfly's wings and ate the body in one gulp.

Anax was a wild animal, wary of humans. Sometimes he hunted and rested in swamps, vast forests, and other wild places. For a dragonfly, though, all the air space ten feet or more above the ground is wilderness. Dragonflies have been seen hunting over the infield during World Series baseball games. As Anax journeyed south, he caught food along highways and over soccer fields and city parks. He spent most of a day patrolling the air above a little park in Savannah, Georgia. People strolled through the park and relaxed in it. Overhead, unnoticed, predators chased prey. Like cheetahs pursuing gazelles on Africa's Serengeti Plain, Anax and other dragonflies killed and ate mosquitoes, midges, and flies.

Anax was thirsty. He looked for water. Near the Savannah park he saw a gleam like sunlight reflected from a pool. He swooped low and hovered just above the surface. Then he darted away. He had mistaken the roof of a car for a pool of water. A dragonfly's vision is terrific at spotting a little insect on the move, yet it can sometimes mistake shiny metal for water. Occasionally female dragonflies lay eggs on the roofs or hoods of automobiles.

After a short flight Anax found water to drink at a pond. Then he hunted the fronts of some buildings, flying a few feet away from the surface. He hovered and probed, darting in and out, catching flies and bees that took flight. Later, on the edge of Savannah, he ate mosquitoes until well after sunset. Then he landed in a sweet gum tree, cleaned the surface of his eyes, and settled down for the night.

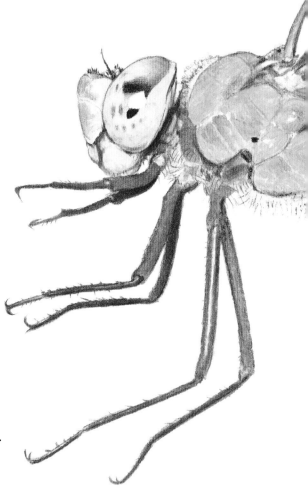

Soon after dawn Anax flew south along the Georgia coast. Once on his long journey he had been carried inland by winds, but a cold front from the northwest had soon pushed him back to the ocean's edge. Travel was easy there.

In the morning a warm breeze blew inland from the ocean. When it struck cooler air over land, the warm air rose. This happened all along the shore. The long mass of rising warm air formed an aerial highway for migrators—birds, monarch butterflies, and dragonflies.

The rising air also carried many small insects aloft. Anax ate well. Despite his long journey, he had added fat reserves for energy. His flight muscles were big and powerful. Anax was in the prime of his life, a fierce predator, a dragon in the sky.

The last signs of his teneral stage had vanished. His green thorax gleamed. His abdomen, once a purplish brown color, had gradually turned a brilliant blue. Within his abdomen there were other changes. His reproductive organs had developed. Anax was ready to mate.

In Bali, Laos, Japan, China, and other Asian nations, dragonflies are valued for their grace and beauty— and as food. Children catch them, sometimes by dipping the end of a narrow stick in sticky sap, then waving the stick in the air. Dragonflies get caught in the sap. They can be grilled, cooked with vegetables, or fried in coconut oil and eaten like candy.

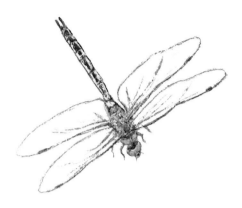

male green darner

So were many other green darners. Their mass migration began to disperse. The darners spread out over Florida, and beyond. They looked for the ponds, swamps, and other quiet waters that female green darners seek for laying eggs. Many dragonflies were also pushed away from Florida's east coast by winds from the remnants of a hurricane in the Atlantic.

In early November, Anax glided down near a pond in south-western Florida. The surroundings were very different from the swamp in western New York where his life had begun. In this region there were dragonflies new to Anax: regal and comet darners, amber-wings, and roseate and slaty skimmers. Much of his food remained the same though. There was a bounty of mosquitoes, crane flies, and other small flying insects. Anax seldom ate anything larger.

As Anax explored along the edge of the pond, a male eastern amberwing dragonfly rose from its perch and rushed toward him. The amberwing was defending a possible egg-laying site. Anax spun in the air and caught the amberwing. It was a small dragonfly, less than half Anax's size. He landed on a twig to eat it.

Anax patrolled the air above the small pond. He flew about twenty feet above the water, but sometimes probed the cattails and other plants close to the surface. These were places where a female green darner would lay eggs. Dragonflies have more than one mate. Sometimes a male finds a female after she has already mated and has begun to lay eggs.

Anax was prepared for mating. His reproductive cells, called sperm, were stored in the ninth segment of his abdomen, close to its tip. He had perched and bent his abdomen double, reaching under to deposit the sperm in a chamber near the front of his abdomen. Once ready, he grew even more eager to find a mate.

A large dragonfly flew into sight, a male green darner. Anax turned and sped straight toward the intruder. There was a clatter of wings as they met in the air. With Anax in hot pursuit both dragonflies disappeared from the pond. In a few moments only Anax returned. He cruised back and forth, back and forth, until darkness fell.

She appeared the next morning—a female green darner. The sides of her abdomen were gray green, not blue, and Anax could see other clues that the newcomer was a female. He hovered near her, then closed in, grasping her thorax from above with his second and third pairs of legs. His front legs gently touched her antennae. She did not resist. They flew together slowly, and then Anax perched on a cattail leaf.

Scientists believe that cold weather fronts, with winds from the northwest, stimulate green darners and a few other species to migrate. A species called the variegated meadowhawk has been seen migrating along the West Coast. In the East, it seems likely that many green darners spread out in Florida and other southern states, where they mate and die. But green darners have been seen flying west along the Gulf coast, and even crossing part of the Gulf of Mexico. How far do they go? The migration of dragonflies holds many mysteries.

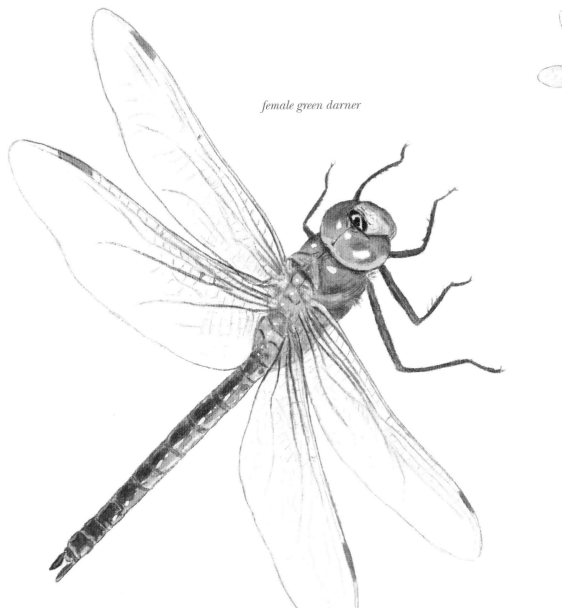

female green darner

OVERLEAF:
a pond in southwestern Florida

male

female

When dragonflies mate, the male
holds the female's head with the tip
of his abdomen while the female
takes sperm from a chamber near the
front of his abdomen.

Anax let go of the female with his feet but quickly gripped the
back of her head with the claspers on the end of his abdomen. She
took hold of his abdomen with her feet, then put the tip of her
abdomen into the chamber where his sperm were stored. Their bodies formed a crude circle or wheel. Anax and his mate stayed in the
wheel position for nearly a half hour. During that time, while Anax
clung to a plant stem and the female clung to him, she received
enough sperm to fertilize hundreds of her eggs. Anax let go of the
female, and for a few moments both darners groomed themselves.
Then they set out, flying together in the tandem position, as she flew
down to the pond's edge and began laying eggs. Anax held the back
of her head with his claspers. He kept alert for danger, and for the
threat of another green darner male seeking a female.

Late in the November afternoon, Anax and the female parted.

She did not reappear the next day. During the following two weeks, Anax mated with several females, as they had with other males.

One day Anax simply rested on top of a cattail seed head. His bright colors had begun to fade, and his wings bore some nicks and a tear from his clashes with other males.

He had eaten less than usual during his mating time. Now that time was over, yet he seemed too tired to hunt.

Hidden beneath the pond's surface were thousands of green darner eggs that Anax had fertilized. In a few days tiny nymphs would hatch from the eggs. Some of the nymphs would survive to emerge in the Florida spring as green darner dragonflies. They would fly north, grow stronger every day, and become fierce dragons in the sky somewhere far, far away.

Anax's life of adventure and danger would soon be over, but not yet. Anax saw something in flight twenty feet away. It was a mosquito. Anax lifted into the air once more. The last thing the mosquito saw was Anax's face.

If you live near an unpolluted pond, marsh, or other wetland, you can catch a dragonfly or damselfly nymph and keep it for a while. You can watch it catch its food and molt. Perhaps you can keep it long enough to see it emerge as an adult, to be set free to fly away.

Remember, though, that some nymphs need several months and sometimes even years in order to mature to adults. Raising one to adulthood can be a long-term project. Keeping one for a few days or weeks will be enough time for you to observe some fascinating dragonfly nymph behavior.

To catch a nymph, you need a small-meshed aquarium net and some sturdy plastic bags that can be sealed shut. Nymphs can usually be found hidden on underwater plants within reach of shore. Sweep the net through the water plants, then look to see what you caught. Illustrations on page 25 show how to tell the nymphs of dragonflies and damselflies apart. If you catch one good-sized nymph, put it in a plastic bag with pond water and some pond weeds. Other smaller insects you catch can be put in separate bags with pond plants. They will be food for the large nymph.

Keep the plastic bags out of direct sunlight while taking them home. The nymph can be kept in a large glass jar or a small glass or plastic aquarium. Fill its container about half full with pond water or tap water that has been allowed to stand for a day (if your water supply is chlorinated). Its home should have a screen cover or other top. Keep the nymph's food supply of small water insects in a separate container. Both containers should also include some Elodea or other aquatic plant stems and leaves.

The nymph should be fed at least one aquatic insect daily. Watch to see it catch and eat its prey. You may also see it jet through the water and discard its old exoskeleton as it molts. Then you can carry it back to its home in the wild and let it go.

If you hunt for a nymph at the right time of the year (which varies with different species), you may catch one that is nearly ready to become an adult. It will have large wing pads on its thorax. It will stop eating shortly before it begins its final molt. Do not cover the nymph's container, and leave a stick or length of screening for the nymph to climb and cling to while it changes to an adult. It must have room to spread its wings and time in which to dry them before you release it outdoors.

nymph container   *food supply container*

To Find Out More

The books and articles listed below range from children's books to scholarly articles in scientific journals. In addition, a wealth of up-to-date information and colorful images of dragonflies and damselflies can be found at the Internet Web sites given on the next page.

Carpenter, Virginia. *Dragonflies and Damselflies of Cape Cod.* Brewster, Mass.: Cape Cod Museum of Natural History, 1991.

Conniff, Richard. "Dragonflies Are an Odd Combination of Beautiful Things," *Smithsonian* (July 1996): 70–81.

Corbet, Philip. *A Biology of Dragonflies.* Chicago: Quadrangle Books, 1963.

Dunkle, Sidney. *Dragonflies through Binoculars.* New York: Oxford University Press, 2000.

Fergus, Charles. "Lord and Master of June," *Science 82* (June 1982): 54–59.

Hutchins, Ross. *The World of Dragonflies and Damselflies.* New York: Dodd, Mead and Company, 1969.

McClung, Robert. *Green Darner: The Story of a Dragonfly.* New York: Morrow Junior Books, 1980.

McLaughlin, Molly. *Dragonflies.* New York: Walker, 1989.

Nicoletti, Frank. "American Kestrel and Merlin Migration Correlated with Green Darner Movements at Hawk Ridge," *The Loon* (Winter 1996–97): 216–20.

O'Toole, Christopher. *The Dragonfly over the Water.* London: Methuen Children's Books, 1988.

Pemberton, Robert. "Catching and Eating Dragonflies in Bali and Elsewhere in Asia," *American Entomologist* (Summer 1995): 97–99.

Peterson, Ivars. "On the Wings of a Dragonfly," *Science News* (August 10, 1985): 90–91.

Russell, Robert, Michael May, Kenneth Soltesz, and John Fitzpatrick. "Massive Swarm Migrations of Dragonflies (Odonata) in Eastern North America," *American Midland Naturalist* (October 1998): 325–42.

Simon, Hilda. *Dragonflies.* New York: Viking, 1972.

Stolzenburg, William. "Hunting Dragonflies: On Safari for the Big Game of the Insect World," *Nature Conservancy* (May–June 1994): 24–29.

Trottier, Robert. "The Emergence and Sex Ratio of *Anax junius* in Canada," *The Canadian Entomologist* (August 1966): 794–98.

Young, Allen. "The Flying Season and Emergence Period of *Anax junius* in Illinois," *The Canadian Entomologist* (August 1967): 886–90.

Dragonfly Web Sites

There are more than two hundred sites on the World Wide Web with information about dragonflies and damselflies (Odonata). Many include photographs of various species. The photographs can help identify dragonfly species across North America.

The variety of information available includes tips on how to photograph dragonflies and images of Odonata on postage stamps from all over the world. Many Web sites report on species that live in various states and regions across North America and in many foreign countries. Some report on research, including study of the mysteries of dragonfly migration.

All of the sites listed below and scores of others can be reached by links from the site of *Ode News*—"an occasional newsletter about dragonflies and damselflies on Cape Cod." Its address is

> http://www.capecod.net/~bnikula/odenews.htm

Digital Dragonflies
> http://www.dragonflies.org/

Odonata Information Network and Web Site
> http://www.afn.org/~iori/

Items of interest to Odonata Enthusiasts
> http://casswww.ucsd.edu/personal/ron/CVNC/odonata/
> index.html

North American Dragonfly Migration Project
> http://members.bellatlantic.net/~dbarber/migrant/mig.html

Index